PIER PRESSURE

DOGG PACK SERIES

EVIE MITCHELL

THUNDER THIGHS PUBLISHING

Editors: Nicole Wilson, Evermore Editing
http://www.evermoreediting.wixsite.com/info
Illustrator: Laras Putri

ACKNOWLEDGEMENT OF COUNTRY

I acknowledge the Traditional Custodians of the lands on which I write, the Ngunnawal people, and pay my respect to elders both past and present.

I acknowledge the continued and deep spiritual relationship of the Australian Aboriginal and Torres Strait Islander peoples' to this land, and their unique cultural and spiritual relationships to the land, waters and seas and their rich contribution to society.

Always was, always will be.

*Bears, Beets, Battlestar Galatica.
Thanks for allowing me to annoy you from now
until eternity.*

James

All I wanted was a week away with friends. A week to sit by the lake, listen to some tunes, and maybe forget for five minutes that my best friend was engaged to a guy I despised.

Well, that was the plan until Hazel called and said she and Mister-I'm-Too-Good-For-Camping had broken up.

Now it's my chance to do something I should have done years ago, turn myself from best friend into boyfriend.

I don't want to be the rebound. I want to be her only.

If only Hazel could see that.

Hazel

Peer pressure. It's the only reasonable explanation for why I'm on this trip.

Oh, that and wanting to escape the judgmental glares of my parents.

After my failed engagement to Mister-I-Don't-Share-Fries, I just want a quiet week away with my friends. Sun, sand, and swimming is the perfect way to mend a bruised heart.

Only... my heart doesn't feel that bruised. In fact, it feels kind of... achy. And excited. And it seems to skip every time James enters the room.

It feels a lot like... love?

CHAPTER 1

Hazel

I stared at the article on my screen.

Disbelief warred with shock as denial hit me like a truck.

This can't be happening.

My phone rang, and without thinking I slid my thumb across the screen answering the call.

"Hello?"

"Hazel Bronze?"

I frowned, not recognizing the voice. "Yes? How did you get this number?"

"This is George Kingly from *Gossip Daily.* Do you have any comments on your ex-fiancé's elopement with Prika Thompson?"

I swallowed, attempting to draw moisture into my desert-like mouth. "No comment."

"Are you sure? Cause it's not every day your fiancé dumps you to get a quickie wedding to Hollywood's sexiest woman."

I cleared my throat, forcing strength behind my words. "No comment."

"But, Hazel. Don't you want to—"

"No comment!" I hit end, tossing my cell into my tote, my hands shaking as I reached for the edge of my desk, gripping it with white knuckles, my eyes once again scanning the article on my computer.

Thompson and Ryder Tie the Knot

It's time to welcome our newest Mr. and Mrs.! Following his breakout debut as Derrick Golland in last year's blockbuster End of Days, alongside our fan favourite actor and director, Robbie Huynh.

Though new to Hollywood, Ricky Ryder has taken the silver screen by storm, capturing the heart of our favorite actress—Prika Thompson. Voted Hollywood's hottest actress three years in a row, Ms. Thompson the pair met on the set of End of Days, sending tongues waggling at their incredible chemistry.

In a surprise announcement overnight, the loved-up pair tied the knot at the famous A Little White Chapel in Vegas. The venue includes five indoor chapels – the Little White, L'Amour, Crystal, Promises and Green Room, as well as an outdoor gazebo, and the historic, world-famous Tunnel of Love Drive-Thru, and has hosted the weddings of stars like Jonas and Sophie Turner, Bruce Willis and Demi Moore, and Frank Sinatra and Mia Farrow.

The wedding came as no shock to friends of the newlyweds.

"They've been dating in secret for months. I've been friends with them for years and never seen them so happy. It's such a relief to know that they can now share this joy with the world."

The two released the following statement on their respective social media accounts.

"Sometimes you just know when you've met your soul mate. We're so blessed to be surrounded by the love of our families and friends. We'll have a proper wedding sometime in the future, but in the meantime—here's to our wonderful future."

We wish the happy couple all the best.

The words on my screen began to swim in front of my eyes as my phone vibrated with another call. I reached down automatically, checking the screen.

Oh, shit.

I braced, answering the call.

"Hello, mother."

"Hazel, I've got all my friends calling me with news of Richard's elopement. What is the meaning of this?"

I sucked in a breath, attempting to calm my racing heart. "Your guess is as good as mine. Yesterday I was speaking to his personal assistant about canapes for the reception. Today I'm looking at—at—at—" I choked, my throat closing.

"You failed, Hazel." She left no room for argument.

I sucked in a breath, my eyes closing as I tried to force the emotions down.

"I know. I'm sorry."

My mother was silent for a long time, her displeasure leaking down the phone line.

"Your father and I will discuss the matter. We will find another appropriate suitor for you. Don't expect a reprieve this time. The wedding will progress quickly. No arguments."

"I understand."

She hung up, the dial tone in my ear a familiar farewell.

Shit.

My body began to shut down, uncontrollable trembles shaking my limbs as the reality of my situation crashed into me.

Shit. Shit. Shit. What am I going to do now?

I fumbled with my phone, scrolling to Ricky's number and hitting call.

Once upon a time, he'd been Richard Gordon Jr., son of one of the richest men in Astipia. Now he was Ricky Ryder—a name he'd adopted upon the advice of his agent when he'd first made it to Hollywood.

Pick up!

"Hello?"

My heart leapt into my throat.

"Ricky, it's Hazel. I just wanted to ask about—"

The phone went dead.

I blinked, pulling it away from my ear to stare down at the screen.

"Fudge." I hit redial, trying again.

"What do you want, Hazel?" He sounded belligerent this time, the sleep gone from his voice, replaced by annoyance.

I sucked in a breath, knowing my fears were about to be realized. "It's true, isn't it? You got married last night?"

There was a long pause.

"Yeah."

My gaze fell to the picture on my computer screen, blinding staring at the picture of Ricky and his new bride as they shared their wedding vows.

"Were you going to tell me?"

"You've read the newspapers?"

"Yes?"

"Then you know."

Hurt bloomed in my chest. "We've been together a long time. Didn't you think I deserved a phone call?"

He huffed out a bitter laugh. "Together? We were an arrangement between parents, Hazel. You've been nothing but a stone around my neck for years."

My eyes drifted closed, tears clogging my throat. "But you were fond of me, weren't you?"

There was another long pause.

"Ricky?"

He sighed heavily. "Look, next time? How about you tell your parents to fuck off and marry someone who'll actually make you happy? Good luck, kid."

And with that, he hung up, shattering my future.

Oh, God. Oh, God. Oh, God! Crabapples and firetrucks!

My phone buzzed, text number six hundred and nineteen lighting my screen.

MOTHER

We have a possible option.
Come home this weekend and
we will discuss.

Dread crept up my spine, my blood running cold.

"Fudge apples."

CHAPTER 2

James

"Oh, shit." Dylan stared at their phone, Ms. Pepper snoozing on their lap.

"What?" Their partner, Meredith asked, looking up from her book. "Is it another Capdashian thing again?"

"It's Kardashian, darling. And no, it's worse." Their gaze lifted from the phone, settling on me. "It's Hazel's fiancé."

I stiffened, knowing shit was about to hit the fan. "Hit me, Dyl."

"The bastard got married last night."

I closed my eyes, my heart heavy.

You knew this was coming.

"To Prika Thompson."

I lurched, my body already in movement before my mind could catch up. I snatched the phone from Dylan, scrolling down the screen.

"Holy fuck. That fucking motherfucker!"

I pulled my phone from my pocket, switching it on and hitting speed dial for Hazel.

"You're meant to be on vacation," she said, her tone accusatory.

"I heard. That fucking bastard. Did he at least call first?"

She sucked in a breath, and it was all the explanation required.

"That motherfucker!"

"James, stop. It—it is what it is. Ricky is— was, who he was. That chapter of my life is done now. It's—it's—it's—" she broke off, her voice breaking.

"Oh, buddy...." I wanted to reach through the phone and wrap her in a tight hug. I wanted to rip my chest open and hand her my heart since I knew hers would be broken.

I love you, Hazel. You deserve better.

"Look, I'll come back tonight. We'll get drunk, watch one of those shitty movies you love, eat from that place that gave us the food poisoning last time we—"

"Absolutely not. You're on vacation for the first time in three years. There is no way I'm allowing you to return to the office. You *or*

Ash," she clarified, knowing us both far too well.

I met my brother's gaze over the table. Millie sat on his lap; her expression stricken.

"Then come here. We'll get some burgers from Pier Pressure. We'll watch that movie you love with the Emma Thompson—"

"House Bunny."

"Yeah, that one. And we'll make sure you forget your woes."

There was a long pause on the other end of the call.

"Please Hazel? It's not the same without you."

It was the truth. Our little pack of four had set up the business—Ash as the brains, me as the hard-ass financial leader, Hazel organizing the shit out of us, and Dylan acting as gatekeeper as we began to grow. Before we'd gone international, we used to take this holiday every year—just the four of us pretending it was a corporate bonding experience when really it was an excuse to relax and unwind in a place with patchy reception.

But we hadn't had a chance to do this in three years, not since we'd gone global and opened the international offices. Since then, it had been nothing but work with the occasional Sunday off.

This year was different what with me buying this lake house, my brother bringing along his fiancé, and Dylan bringing Meredith. Hazel had declined, deciding to stay in the city and concentrate on planning her wedding. We'd only been here for a few hours but nothing had felt right without her here.

"Okay," she whispered, her voice tight. "I'll be there tomorrow."

"Promise? Or do I need to call in a bodyguard or two to wrestle you up here?"

There was a small thread of amusement in her tone when she answered. "No, I'll be there."

My body relaxed a little hearing it.

"Okay, we'll see you bright and early tomorrow."

"Thanks, James. I... I'll be alright."

"I know, buddy. Just get here."

She hung up and I looked at the phone, my heart aching.

"Is she coming?" Millie asked, breaking my thoughts of revenge against her fiancé.

"Yeah, she'll be here tomorrow."

Ash considered me over Millie's head, his gaze far too knowing.

"Well," Dylan swept one hand out to encompass the wilderness around us. "If there was any place to recover from a broken heart the wilds of Lovers Lake is it."

I looked out at the view, taking in the gently lapping water over which the sun was setting.

"Dylan?"

"Yes, my darling?" They asked Meredith.

"Shut up." She flicked a hand my way. "The man is clearly torn about this predicament. To get this heart's desire the woman of his dreams had to be hurt."

I blanched, staring at Meredith. "How did you—"

"I'm a psychologist. It's my job to understand human behaviour."

"Not to mention," Dylan drawled, rolling their eyes. "*Everyone* knows. You're not exactly subtle, James."

"Well, everyone except Hazel," Ash murmured, nuzzling Millie's neck and making her laugh.

"Shit." I ran a hand through my hair. "What do I do now, oh bearers of wisdom?"

"Woo her, of course," Meredith stated it as if it were obvious. She turned the page in her romance novel.

"Woo her?"

She sighed, looking up from her book, her frizz of red curly hair waving gently in the breeze. "Yes, James, woo her. Mend her broken heart by giving her your own."

Her words were scarily similar to my own thoughts.

"What if she doesn't want me?" I asked, my voice hoarse as I admitted my deepest fear.

"Then at least you tried."

With that, Meredith went back to her book, licking a finger to turn the page.

"So, on that note, anyone for more cocktails?" Dylan asked, holding up a bottle of vodka.

I shoved my glass across the table. "Better make it a double."

I'd need all the courage I could get.

CHAPTER 3

Hazel

James Dogg looked like a boxer—even was one, back in college—tall, broad, with muscles upon muscles he looked less academic and more *I'll fuck you up*. But as Chief Financial Officer for one of the fastest-growing green-tech firms in the world, he often had to cover himself up, toning down the rugged masculinity in exchange for a sheen of civility.

But here at the lake, there were no business meetings. No suits. Nothing but James in board shorts with his strong arms held wide open in welcome.

God how I needed a hug.

James helped me out of the car then

hauled me up and into his arms, crushing me in a tight clutch. I closed my eyes, breathing in his familiar scent, memorizing the feel of this, allowing the familiarity of him to comfort me.

Safe.

"Are you okay, buddy?"

His question was so quintessentially James that tears stung the back of my eyes.

"I—" Words caught in my throat, nausea swirling in my stomach as I tried to say that I was okay. That everything was fine. That he didn't need to worry about me.

Liar.

He pulled back a fraction, his face darkening as his gaze swept across my face. "What the actual *fuck*, Hazel? How the fuck could he do that to you?"

Thank God someone said it.

"I don't know."

James pulled me back into him, his arms tight around me.

"I'm sorry."

I'm not.

The words hovered on the tip of my tongue, the truth terrifying.

"We'll get you through this," James promised, squeezing me. "A week away from cameras, phones, and work is just what you need. We'll swim and hike and eat until we're about to burst."

A small spark lit in my belly, chasing away a fraction of the icy dread that had lived in me since reading the wedding article. Such was the power of James. He was my oldest friend, and one of my most favourite people in the world. When he and Ash, his brother, had started Dogg Wood Industries, they'd asked me to come on as their office manager. Since our humble beginnings in their dad's garage, my title had changed over the years, but my duty never had—it was my life's purpose to help make James a success.

"I'd love that," I croaked, my throat raw with unshed tears. "Thanks."

"Any time, you know that."

He pulled back, his dark gaze searching my face as his cheeks took on a ruddy colour. "There's just uh, that is to say, well...."

I braced for more bad news.

"With everyone here, I'm afraid we don't have any spare beds."

My heart seized. "Do I need to leave?"

"Fuck no." James shook his head, emphasising his words. "But you'll have to share with me, if that's okay?"

"Share as in...?"

"It's a double, so there's plenty of space.

And we can build a pillow wall that goes down the middle if that makes you more comfortable. Think of it like that time in Vegas when they put us in the honeymoon suite."

Memories of that night crashed through my fog of self-pity, chasing the clouds away.

Vodka. Tequila. Laughter.

Temptation.

It had been months after we'd gotten the patent and approvals for the world's first green battery. We'd launched at a trade show, borrowing money from Jay Wood—James and Ash's brother—to fund the big reveal. Hours after launch we'd been inundated with offers from everyone from tech juggernauts to Silicon Valley startups. It had been the start of our rocket to the top.

We hadn't expected to spend more than two days in Vegas, so we'd been left without accommodation as I rushed to change flights and find us a hotel while we were wined and dined by everyone from CEOs down.

After one particularly successful dinner, we'd gone out to celebrate, winding up checking into our hotel in the early hours of the following morning. We'd discovered that the only room available was the honeymoon suite, but drunk on joy, we'd taken it.

Ash had immediately crashed out on the

couch, leaving James and me the bed. We'd laughed, building a pillow wall between us, chatting about the possibilities these offers could bring to the company. As we'd lay under the same blanket, something strange had happened. I'd turned to see James looking at me, gaze serious in the dim light of the room.

"Are you okay?" I'd whispered into the dark.

"No."

My heart had caught at the pain in his voice.

"What can I do to help?"

James had remained silent for a long moment, our gaze holding.

"Are you still marrying Ricky?"

"Of course."

He'd nodded once, his expression shuttering. "I hope he'll make you happy, Hazel."

For a moment, just before he'd rolled away from me, I'd caught a flash of something in his face that had made me ache all over. It had left me shivery and warmly lethargic in a way, I hadn't ever felt before. In a way I'd never experienced with Ricky.

I'd taken his cue, rolling over to give him my back and searched for sleep. Since that night there'd never been another moment like that between us. But I'd always wondered what had caused that pain in his eyes.

Or perhaps the better question was who.

"As long as we don't wake up to Ash puking on the love seat, I think I can handle sharing a bed with you."

James barked out a laugh, draping an arm over my shoulder to guide me into the house. "No promises. The man still can't hold his liquor."

I chuckled, tipping my head back to look up at the large lake house.

Ash, James, and I were from Capricorn Cove. We'd lived next door to each other, and I'd taken them under my wing when they'd moved into the street. They were adopted brothers—two of six if you included their former foster brother and newest sister—and the family was colloquially known as the Dogg Pack. For years I'd wished I could be a part of their rough and ready family as they'd tumbled down hills, climbed trees, and lived with skinned knees.

My mother had been horrified by their presence in the affluent neighbourhood and had done everything in her power to get the Home Owners Association to kick them out. Unlucky for her, Will Dogg—James and Ash's adopted Dad—had inherited the land from his parents, who had lived there for years before the millionaires had moved into the surrounding areas. Their house was one of those old farm-ranch-style things, and their dad still lived there with his new wife and their daughter, surrounded by trees and failed tree forts.

The lake house was a new acquisition James had purchased on a whim. His apartment was in Wellesley Falls, the city closest to our small town and the location of Dogg Wood Industries headquarters. But living in the city had its downsides—particularly when you were a mountain man at heart. While it had seemed like an impulsive purchase, I'd caught James scanning real estate listings for months before he'd finally made an offer.

"Leave your bags, we'll grab them later."

"Where is everyone?" I asked as he led me up the short path.

"Fishing. Apparently, Dylan wanted to learn, and their partner was only too happy to accommodate."

"You know I love Meredith, but the woman honestly terrifies me. She isn't who I would have picked for them, but I am so glad she came along. They're adorable together."

"Agreed." James caught my hand, helping

me over a broken stair. "Sorry, the place needs work," he said, his tone apologetic.

"And a clean," I laughed, catching sight of the dirty windows along the deck.

"But it's a good investment, wait until you see the view."

He led me around the giant deck to the rear of the house, my breath catching.

"Oh, James."

Trees provided shade on either side of the deck, but the land directly in front of the deck had been cleared to make way for a long stretch of lawn, broken only by a small boat shed and a seating area complete with an ancient fire pit. At the far end of the lawn sat Lovers Lake, the view magnificent.

"This is stunning."

He laughed, running a hand through his unruly hair. "It will be. It needs work, but I couldn't say no. I mean... just look at the view."

The water sparkled in the clear sunshine, inviting me to stroll down and take a swim. The shoreline was a mix of sand and pebbles, perfect for exploring or lazing around sun-baking while reading a good book. There was even a little pier that took you out a fair way into the lake, perfect for swimming or horsing around.

Oh, sure. The lawn needed a good tidy,

and the deck required some repairs. But seeing how the weeds warred with a riot of wildflowers, I couldn't help but think that the beautiful wilderness somehow fit James' personality.

This is exactly the house I would have purchased for him.

"So, what do you think?"

I want to get married here.

I shoved the thought away as regret and hurt stabbed at my chest.

"It's perfect. This is exactly the home I would have chosen for you."

"You say that, but you haven't seen the kitchen or bathrooms yet."

I laughed, giving him a little hip bump. "Do I want to know?"

He leaned in, his hand settling on my lower back. James' warm breath brushed the shell of my ear as he whispered, "No."

He pulled back, sending me a wink.

"Come on, let's start in the heart of the home—the kitchen."

James shoved open a sliding deck door, the rollers protesting as they slid along the rusty track.

"Oh, dear, that's not a good—" I choked as I stepped through the doors, my eyes widening as I attempted to absorb the disaster before me.

"What in the world were these people thinking?"

James laughed as I slowly began to spin, taking in the clash of colour and patterns.

"Lime green and wood veneer cabinets with—" I gasped. "Is that *carpet* in the kitchen?"

James doubled over, his laughter preventing him from answering.

"Oh my God, James. Is that a hypnosis wall?" I raised my hand to my eyes, blocking my view. "I actually can't look at it. It's making me sick." A lamp in the corner of the room caught my attention. "There's a lava lamp?"

"It came with the house," he managed to get out, tears now running down his face.

"Dear Lord above, we're gonna need industrial strength cleaning products." I pointed at the velour sofa. "This came with the house, didn't it?"

He nodded, a wide grin on his face.

"James, you gotta burn it. It's totally been jizzed on. There have either been orgies in this house, or a serial killer lived here. Either way, it's gotta go."

He bent over, his whole body shaking with laughter as I began to walk around the house, pointing at the crazy eccentricities present.

"What on earth is that?" I asked, pointing

at a doorknob sticking out from a wall in the hall.

"The doorway to our bedroom." He twisted the knob, the hidden door sliding open to reveal a room I could only describe as nightmarish.

"James." I reached out, bracing myself against the wall, my body physically unable to hold me up. "James, what have you done?"

He chuckled, pushing me into the room, gesturing at the wallpaper. "Isn't it great?"

"No, this house needs a priest. We need holy water and an exorcist, stat."

The room had the creepiest wallpaper I'd ever seen. It was the same print over and over, a doll playing with her toys, her head turned towards you. There had to be about fifty of them scattered around the room, each with their dead eyes and creepy grin trained on me.

"This had to have been a nursery," James said, fingering a piece of loose wallpaper.

"God help those children." I moved closer to James, pressing into his side to rise on tiptoe and whisper in his ear. "The walls have eyes."

"Yeah, it's some Mona Lisa kind of shit," James agreed, wrapping an arm around me. "Don't worry. I'll protect you."

"I'm not sleeping in here. Not unless we cover every single one of their eyes."

James reached into his back pocket, pulling

two markers out. "Somehow, I knew you'd say this."

"James!" I snatched a marker with a laugh. "You knew!"

"Of course I did. You can't be best friends with a person for twenty years and not know when they're gonna be petrified of wallpaper."

I rolled my eyes, pulling the cap off with my teeth and beginning to draw a box around the face of the demon doll. "Just get to work, Dogg. I do wanna sleep tonight."

"Yes, ma'am." James fell in beside me. "Siri, play wallpaper playlist."

"Playing wallpaper playlist."

I began to laugh as a man began to sing about wallpaper roses. Every time the singer said roses, James shouted dolls.

"Oh my God, stop! I can't take it!"

He grinned as the song wrapped up. "It's good to see you smiling, Hazel."

The smile on my face and the laughter in my belly didn't waiver. "It's good to be smiling again."

With his phone finally playing some decent music, we continued to cover the eyes of the dolls.

CHAPTER 4

James

I watched Hazel dancing with Meredith on the deck in the moonlight, her body swaying slightly out of time to the music. She was three sheets to the wind drunk and I had zero regrets about getting her there.

She's gorgeous.

Long legs, curvy body, button nose. Hazel had deep auburn hair that fell to just above her shoulders, the colour startling against her pale skin. She burned easily, and I noticed that while the sun had set hours before, a faint pink had begun to touch her skin.

Aloe before bed.

"Oh!" Hazel turned to Dylan. "He never shared his fries!"

Dylan shook their head sadly. "Mister-I-Don't-Share-Fries. Adding it to the list."

They pulled out their phone, jotting the nickname down.

At some point during the night, Dylan had suggested we start a shit list about Ricky. Hazel had jumped on it, all of us adding to it as the night wore on.

"And how about Mister-never-called-me-the-right-surname?" Hazel asked, then spun off to begin dancing with Meredith once more.

"I don't understand," Millie slurred to Ash, who was sitting beside me. "I thought her name is Hazel Green."

"It is. She changed it. It's a long sad story, sweetness, go back to sleep."

"Shhokay." Millie promptly lay her head on his shoulder and closed her eyes. Within moments she began to snore softly, the warm day and rich wine catching up with her.

The song finished and I stood, ignoring Dylan as they sent me a knowing look.

"COME ON, HAZEL, BEDTIME."

"Did we get all the eyes?" She asked, swaying a little as she tried to focus on me.

"Yep, all the creepy eyes are covered."

She shuddered, shaking her head. "This house is weird."

"That's why I bought it." I placed a hand on her back, beginning to gently guide her off the deck. "Everyone needs a story of their renovation woes."

"Story? You'll have a whole saga!"

I chuckled, wincing a little when we walked inside.

"How is it your kitchen looks worse at night?" Hazel asked, shaking her head at the glowing kitchen.

"It's glow-in-the-dark linoleum."

"That's a thing?"

"Apparently. Either that or it's radioactive."

"In which case we better take turns sleeping."

I raised an eyebrow in question.

"In case the dolls come alive and try to kill us while we sleep."

I laughed, fumbling for the hidden door. "Don't worry, Hazy, I'll keep you safe."

"Do you have a gun?"

"Better. I have the power of being a mediocre middle-aged, white man. We're invincible."

I laughed as she lost her shit, enjoying watching her bending over double, her laughing that weird level of hilarity where you look like a gasping sea lion.

"You're silly," she told me, wiping tears from her eyes. "And you're also *not* mediocre."

I shrugged, ignoring her comment. "You need help getting changed?"

She shook her head. "I'm okay. Where's my stuff?"

I pointed at the suitcase in the corner. Hazel bent, digging through her things as I went into the small ensuite, searching for the aloe.

"Hazel, I—" I dropped the bottle, stumbling to a halt in the doorway, my gaze locked on the naked woman standing in the middle of my bedroom.

This has to be a dream.

"What are you—?"

"Make love to me, James."

I was tempted to pinch myself to make sure this wasn't a dream.

"What? Why?"

The woman of my dreams spread her arms wide, bearing herself to me. "Because I deserve an epic love story and I'll never get one."

For a moment all I could do was gaze at her freckled skin, at the yards of curves and planes that were bared to me. My body reacted to this unexpected gift.

Sweet mother of all that is holy, she's more perfect than I've ever imagined.

For fucking years I'd jerked my cock off to scenarios like this. To images of Hazel naked and needy before me, her sweet body welcoming mine.

She's drunk. And hurting. Don't do it, James.

The reality of our situation snapped me back into place.

"Let's get you to bed."

At my endearment her face crumbled, her knees buckling as she began to fall to the floor.

I caught her, scooping her up and carrying her to the bed where her pjs were scattered across the bedclothes. I quickly wrapped her in a robe and then pulled her tight into me.

"Talk to me."

She pressed her face against my chest, her body heaving with sobs, and tears running down her face.

"Why doesn't anyone love me?"

Her question shattered my heart.

"I do, Hazel. I love you. Ash loves you. Dylan. A million people love you, babe. You know that. Ricky is a fucking idiot for leaving you. You deserve better. You deserve a man who'll treat you like a princess."

I'd treat you like a Queen. I'd hold you close and never let you go, Hazel.

She sobbed harder, clutching herself to me, her tears finally cracking through my raging arousal.

"Oh, buddy...." I hugged her close, rocking us as she cried. After a long, long time Hazel finally quieted, her body relaxing in my arms.

"Hazel?"

She snuggled into me, her eyes closed, jaw slack as she slept.

For a moment I gazed down at her familiar face, once again struck by how beautiful this woman was.

"I've been in love with you since you were eight and climbed through the hedge to ask if I wanted a cookie. This might be breaking your heart, but I've never been happier. Not because you're hurting, never that, babe. I'm so fucking happy that I finally have a chance to win your heart." I leaned down, pressing a kiss to her forehead. "I'm coming for you, Hazel. Speak now if you don't want me."

Her only answer was a small breathy sigh.

With a grin I lifted up, walking around the bed juggling her in my arms until I could peel back the covers, gently placing her down on the cool sheet. I double-checked her robe, ensuring she was covered before moving to my own side of the bed. With regret, I wedged a pillow between us, frustrated by the distance it created but knowing Hazel would expect it when she woke in the morning.

"Goodnight, future wife."

CHAPTER 5

Hazel

"I hate you."

Dylan laughed, their eyes dancing in delight. "Do you? Really?"

I squinted up at James as he placed a heaped pile of food on the table. "And you."

The idiot had the gall to shoot me a grin.

Millie, who was slumped beside me, groaned her head in her hands. "Who thought vodka was a good idea?"

Meredith reached for a pancake, giving a shrug that sent her curly hair bobbing. "My Russian ancestors loved a good drinking session."

Millie tossed a blueberry at Meredith. "Hangovers are part of the reason the US and

Russia have been at war. You can't bring this kind of chemical weapon into the country and not warn people."

"Bacon anyone?" Ash plopped a platter piled high with crispy strips.

"Grease is good," I muttered, reaching for a piece.

"What's on today's agenda?" Ash asked, taking a seat at the table.

"Dylan and I are off to a spa day at the Lovers Lake lodge," Meredith said, sending Dylan a wink. "We'll come back relaxed from our heads to our toes."

"Painkillers and a nap by the lake for me," Millie muttered, holding out her glass for Ash to fill.

"I was thinking of taking the boat out." James sent me a questioning look. "You wanna come?"

That strange little warm feeling lit in my belly. "Only if you promise to feed me burgers."

A grin stretched across his face. "I promise."

From inside the house, a phone rang, the ring tone familiar.

"Booger." I shoved up from my seat, sprinting inside to answer it.

"Hello?"

"Hazel, where are you?" My mother's sharp tone cut through my lingering drowsiness.

"I'm—" I hesitated, unsure of how much to reveal. "I'm working."

She scoffed, her derision practically dripping down the phone line. "Working? It's Saturday, Hazel. What do you take me for, an idiot? I sent a car around to your house and you weren't there. You're due for lunch in two hours. If you leave now, you just might get here in time for us to make you presentable."

My gut began to churn, saliva flooding my mouth. "I'm not coming."

"Not—? Unacceptable. We have John Falladay coming for lunch. He's single and perfectly willing to entertain the idea of you as his wife. This act of rebellion must stop if you're going to marry."

I knew she was right. I knew I needed to hitch my wagon to whoever the best option at the time happened to be.

I just didn't want to.

"I... I'll see you at lunch."

"Don't be late."

My mother hung up, leaving me a shaking, emotional mess.

First Ricky and now this?

"Hazel? Is everything alright?"

I turned around to find James watching me from the doorway.

"Was it Ricky?"

I shook my head, my heart giving a weird flutter at the sight of him. "No, it was Mother."

His face pinched. "What did she want?"

"I need to go to lunch. They...." I couldn't get the words out about my potential suitor. "They have someone they want me to meet."

His lips pressed into a thin line, his rugged face taking on a scary look.

"You absolutely have to go?"

I nodded, biting the inside of my cheek to keep from crying.

He was silent for a moment. "Then we'll have burgers for dinner."

I locked my knees, relief making them weak. "Thanks, James. I—"

"And I'm coming."

I froze. "What?"

"I'll come to lunch. Text Heidi and tell her to set a spare place."

I blinked at the mention of my parent's housekeeper. "But why would you—"

"I'm not sending you into the viper's den alone." He closed the distance to me, his hand reaching out to cup my face, his beautiful eyes capturing mine, our gazes holding. "I've got your back, Hazel. Always have. Always will."

Something hovered between us in that moment. Perhaps it was years of shared memories and history. Perhaps it was that being at the lake house had removed us from the roles we'd adopted over the years, breaking down the barriers that time and status had built between us.

Either way, when I looked at James I didn't see a friend or a boss—I saw a man.

A man who makes my heart skip.

I reached out, wrapping my arms around him, giving him a tight squeeze.

"Thank you."

"Any time."

CHAPTER 6

James

"Are you sure you want to go in there?" This wasn't at all the start to our vacation that I'd envisioned. Dressed in a button-up, collared shirt with crisply pressed beige pants, I felt less relaxed and more like I was about to enter piranha invested waters.

Hazel smoothed her palms down her thighs, straightening the material on the skirt of her dress. "Yes."

Her answer didn't sound convincing but I took her at her word.

"Alright, let's get this over with. I'm craving a beer and a burger and God knows what your parents will be serving for lunch."

Hazel chuckled then sobered as the door opened, Heidi standing in the doorway.

"I guess that's our hurry up."

I caught

Hazel's hand, giving it a squeeze. "I'm here for you, Hazy. Whatever you need."

She sent me a grin, returning my squeeze. "Thanks, Jamesie. I love you."

I knew her declaration was love as in friendship, but it didn't stop my body from reacting. Need surged in my bloodstream, my body tensing, my cock hardening.

Fuck.

I pulled away, roughly shoving the door open. "Let's get this over with."

Heidi met us at the door, her hands wringing in her apron.

"Hi Heidi," Hazel greeted. "Are they in the dining room?"

"They're on the terrace, Miss. And a word of warning." She leaned in, her wrinkled face creasing into a frown. "They're determined to see the matter settled today."

Matter?

I glanced at Hazel, alarmed to find the colour in her face had drained away.

"Hazel, what—"

"James, Hazel. We're so pleased you could join us." Her mother shifted Heidi to the side, stepping out to clasp me in an emotionless hug.

"Hey, Mrs Green. Thanks for having me."

"Of course." She pulled away, turning to Hazel, her lips pursing.

Hazel looked nothing like her mother— where she was soft, Mrs Green was sharp.

"Come, we're out on the terrace."

She turned on her heel without greeting Hazel, disappearing into the house.

I caught Hazel's hand, linking our fingers as we walked.

"What are you—"

I gave her hand a squeeze, cutting off her question. "I'm looking out for you, babe."

She blinked up at me, stumbling along as we followed her mother out to the terrace.

"Hazel," her stepdad pushed up from the table, his arms wide as he closed the short distance to greet us. "And James. Wonderful to see you both."

The man gave Hazel a quick hug then held out a hand for me to shake. "I heard you're getting ready to float. Congratulations, James. I'd have never imagined the success you boys have managed to achieve."

Dogg Wood Industries was scheduled to become a publicly-traded company within the next six months.

"Thank you, David. Shall we sit?" I asked, gesturing to the table.

"Yes, let's. Heidi, grab these two kids a drink, yeah?"

The housekeeper disappeared back inside, returning a moment later with two pitchers of drink as we settled at the table.

"I thought someone was joining us," Hazel remarked, frowning at the four places.

"About that," Dawn cleared her throat, holding her glass out for Heidi to fill. "When we heard James was coming, we felt it best to keep our party to the four of us." Mrs Green turned her gaze on me, her expression one I could only describe as wolfish.

Uh-oh.

It took them until the second course to finally get down to business. David leaned back in his chair, his hands knotting over his stomach as he considered me from across the table.

"Now James, I'm sure you're familiar with Hazel's little predicament."

I cocked an eyebrow in question. "Predicament? You mean Ricky the bastard running off without even a sorry?"

David and Dawn exchanged a look.

"Hazel, would you like to tell him?"

Hazel's gaze was trained on her plate, her face pale.

"Tell me what?"

David leaned forward. "Hazel?"

My best friend in the world, the woman I considered closer to me than anyone else looked up from her meal, her expression stricken.

"James, I—" She broke off, her breath catching.

"Tell me, Hazel. You can tell me."

"She has to get married," David finally said, his tone gruff. "Either she gets married or we lose Bronze Pharmaceuticals."

My gaze flicked around the table; this statement was so outrageous that I had no words.

"What?"

"Now that Richard, or should I say Ricky? Well, now that the Gordon boy has married the actress, I'm afraid we've lost the promised investment from his family. Without it, the family business will go bust before the end of the year." David sipped on his mimosa; his gaze locked on me. "We'll be putting about twenty-five hundred people out of a job."

A dull roar began to sound in my ears.

"Why are you telling me this?"

"Because we'd like to offer you Hazel's hand in marriage. In exchange for a financial contribution to keep the business afloat, of course. It's either marriage or we'll be forced to sell. And Hazel here will be the first Bronze child in three generations to have lost the family business."

Dawn's matter-of-fact tone hit me like a punch to the solar plexus.

Hello? 1863? This is the future. Women's rights are calling.

I shoved to my feet, reaching out to haul Hazel along with me.

"Come on," I barked, turning my back to the table, barely able to contain the rage boiling inside me.

"James! Where are you going?" Dawn called as I began to stalk away, Hazel tripping along beside me.

"Away from you." I paused at the doorway, turning to peg them both with an icy glare. "Don't call me. Don't talk to me. And don't you *ever* try and sell your daughter again. If I hear one word of you shopping her around you won't even have until the end of the year. Fuck you, and fuck the cesspit you both crawled out of."

"Now see here!"

I turned my back, pulling Hazel along behind me. "Let's go."

She glanced up at me as we pulled away, my hands white-knuckling the steering wheel.

"What?" I barked, frustrated anger still sizzling under my skin.

"I just wish I'd recorded that."

"Recorded what?"

"You tell my mom and stepdad to fuck off." A small smile stole across her lips, gaining traction until she began to giggle. "Did you see her face? I thought she was about to have a heart attack."

I was too fucking ragey to find the humour. "They deserved it."

"I know." She chuckled, leaning back in her seat. "Shall we get burgers?"

I made a right turn at the T-junction. "Yes. And a fucking beer."

Hazel laughed, reaching out to pat me on my thigh, my cock throbbing at her innocent touch.

"I'll buy the first round, Jamesie."

CHAPTER 7

There's something wrong with James.
I stole another fry from his pile, enjoying the perfectly cooked potato.

"You know," I said, reaching out to grab another one and swipe it through some sauce. "You're the only person in the world who shares their fries with me."

James looked up from where he'd been brooding into his beer bottle. "What?"

"It's why I like you." I stole another. "You share."

"You know I always order extra just for you, right?"

I grinned, popping the fry in my mouth. "Liar. You eat just as much as me."

He grinned, reaching out to steal an onion ring from my plate. "Sharing is caring, babe."

There it is again.

I tipped my head to one side, considering James as he munched on the onion ring.

Since when does he call me babe?

"What?" he asked, glancing down at his shirt. "Do I have something on me?"

I shook my head. "No. It's just...."

How does one ask their best friend if they're more than just protective of you? How do you ask him if he might be...attracted to you?

"Just?" James asked with a grin.

"Nothing." I looked down at the remnants of my burger.

"Hazel, talk to me. What's wrong?"

I glanced up, finding James' gaze trained on me.

What's wrong? How about the fact that you went all caveman on my parents? I mean, it was great but it also felt... intimate. Like a lover protecting their woman.

"I want to do the right thing," I said finally, shoving any romantic feelings deep down inside me. "As much as I want to tell my parents where to shove it, I have to think about the business. There are people's jobs on the line."

James fingered the label of his beer bottle, his expression pensive.

"Remind me again why you took on David's name after your dad died?"

I swallowed. "You know why."

James leaned forward, his gaze piercing. "Humour me."

I looked down at my hands. "David wanted me to be a Green so I could inherit his money. He's sterile. Without any heirs, the trust set aside for his children would go to the extended family."

"You were due to inherit it when you turned twenty-five. I always assumed you did and were just helping me out for fun. But after today...." James trailed off. "What happened to the trust, Hazy?"

I closed my eyes, my head dropping forward. "I gave it to David to invest in my father's company. He said it would fail without it."

James frowned, his lips pressing into a thin line. "Did he?"

I gave a helpless shrug. "I assumed he had. But then they said that I needed to marry Ricky because the company was failing." Tears stung the back of my eyes. "That company is all I have left of my dad. After I can't run it, I know that. I'm not experienced enough. Hell, I'm not even interested in medicine." I sucked in a breath. "But it's my last connection to dad."

My father has been the kind of guy everyone liked. Charismatic, funny, and down to earth, he'd married my mother after she'd fallen pregnant. I'd known their marriage was on the rocks for years, and that the only reason he was staying with her was for me. His death had come as a shock. My mother's swift remarriage had not. Less than six months after my father had been laid in the ground, David, my father's former vice-president, and Mom had said I do in a fancy wedding paid for by the income my father's company had generated. A company he'd built from the ground up through blood, sweat, and tears.

I missed him every day and mourned the fact I'd given in, changing my name all to keep a part of him alive.

A part that might fail despite your efforts.

"So, they've used up your trust and are considering selling the company?"

I nodded, feeling miserable.

"And to save the company they're asking you to...?"

"Marry someone rich enough to bail it out."

James stared at me over the picnic table.

"Why didn't you ask me?"

I blinked. "What?"

"You'd marry Ricky—a piece of shit but you wouldn't entertain the thought of marrying me?"

I stared at James, stunned at his question.

"I-I-I, I couldn't ask that of you. I couldn't sentence you to a loveless marriage. You deserve your happily ever after, James."

He considered me for a moment, his expression unreadable. Finally, he opened his mouth, asking a question that sent me reeling.

"What if my happily ever after is you?"

CHAPTER 8

James

I watched Hazel process my words, her eyes growing wide, her expression shocked.

"W-w-what?"

Now or never, James.

"What if you're my happily ever after?" I leaned across the table, capturing her hand and entwining our fingers. "What if I married you?"

Hazel sucked in a breath, her fingers flinching. "What? What are you saying?"

"Marry me, Hazel."

Her head began to shake slowly back and forth, picking up speed.

"No. No. No. No! No. You don't know what you're saying. You're just being nice."

I shook my own head. "I'm not. I can promise you, I'm absolutely not."

A flush crept up her neck, red suffusing her cheeks. "You need to stop, James. You can't say things like this to me. It's not okay."

"Say what? That I love you? That I've loved you for years? How about the fact that I want you, Hazel? You're the most beautiful woman I've ever seen. Do you have any idea how freaking hard it is to keep away from you?"

She pulled her hand free and shoved to her feet. "Stop it. You can't marry me just to save me! I'm not—you can't—we can't—you're just—" she stuttered to a stop, her head shaking once more. "I have to go."

"Go? Go where?"

"Just... I just need some space." She snatched her bag, then took off, heading for the car park.

"Hazel! Wait! Shit." I scrambled to scoop up our rubbish, tossing it in the bins, my gaze tracking her movement. She was headed for one of the trails, her body jerky, her shoulders heaving.

She's crying.

Whipping myself wouldn't do any good, I needed to fix this.

I raced after her, catching up to Hazel on the trail.

"Hazel, stop!"

I pulled the car keys from my pocket, handing them to her, attempting to ignore her tear-stained cheeks.

"Here. Get yourself home safely."

She looked down at the keys in her hand. "What about you?"

I reached out, wrapping her in a hug. "I'll find my way home. Just take the time you need to process, okay?" I pulled back, searching her face. "I love you, Hazy. As a friend, as a woman, and as the best person I know. If you don't feel anything for me that's okay." I gave her a rueful smile. "I have a lifetime of experience with unrequited love."

She opened her mouth but no words came out.

"I'll see you at home."

I turned on my heel and performed the most difficult manoeuvre of my life—leaving Hazel behind.

CHAPTER 9

Hazel

I stood out on the deck with Dylan, both of us silent as we watched the moon slowly move across the sky.

Ash and Millie had turned in hours ago, leaving Dylan, Meredith, and I to wait for James' return.

Where are you?

"You know he's been in love with you for years." Dylan's soft statement felt like a stab to my chest.

"If he is then why didn't he say anything?"

Dylan sighed, reaching out to squeeze my hand. "Well, for one you were engaged. And for another, because the man is an idiot. He didn't think—doesn't think—he'll ever be good enough for you."

I shook my head. "What do you mean not good enough for me? James is incredible."

"Babe." Dylan tipped their head to one side, giving me a serious stare. "The man was abandoned at a roadside diner as a kid. He bounced around the system for years before Will took him in. His first real home was Will. He didn't feel like he was a part of the Dogg Pack for a long time." Dylan lifted a hand, waving it to encompass the lake house. "The guy has more money than some small countries, he could have any home in the world and he chooses a run-down barely inhabitable dump. He doesn't feel worthy of all this, Hazel. He's never felt worthy of his place in the family, his place in the company, or his place in your life."

I sucked in a breath. "How do you know this?"

Dylan grinned, their teeth flashing in the moonlight. "Meredith is rubbing off on me."

"In the best of ways," the woman said, coming up behind us. She draped herself over Dylan, pressing a kiss to their cheek. "Bed, honey?"

"Mmhmm, in a second." Dylan squeezed Meredith's arm but their gaze was still on me. "The ball is in your court, Hazy. The man wants nothing more than to sweep you off your feet. He wants to kiss you and love you for the rest of his days. All you need to do is decide if you're willing to let that happen."

They stood, wrapping their arm around Meredith, pressing a kiss to her cheek. "Come, darling. Let's retire and leave this munchkin to her brooding."

Meredith sent me a grin. "You'll be okay, Hazel. Just listen to your heart."

"Oh, a Roxette reference! I love a good power ballad." Dylan started humming, swaying with Meredith.

"Come on, silly. Let's head to bed."

With Dylan still humming, they left me alone on the deck to do exactly as they'd said— brood. Or, more precisely, brood while reconsidering every single memory I had of James.

His declaration had left me spinning. How did one fall in love with their best friend and just... not tell them? How did one survive knowing they were in love with them and yet that person was engaged to someone else?

Or not so engaged anymore.

And therein lay the issue. For years I'd viewed James through the prism of 'engaged woman'. I'd boxed him firmly into the friend zone, never allowing myself to even consider if I had romantic feelings for him.

I now felt a little like Pandora's box—once open, nothing could ever be stuffed back in.

But do you love him?

I just didn't know. There was an agony of frustration at the realization.

There had been times in my life when I'd been attracted to James, but I'd assumed those times had long passed. Who we were now didn't reflect the childish feelings I'd held for him once upon a time—feelings that had matured and changed, shifting into what I had thought was friendship, no more, no less.

But what if you were lying to yourself? What if those feelings were there all along?

Re-examining our life, re-examining every interaction, I could see it. James gently brushing my hair from my cheek. Me bringing him lunch when he was pulling a weekender. The shared holidays. The late-night text messages. The private jokes that no one but us understood.

The fact you never fully committed to Ricky.

I sucked in a breath, the cool night air raising the hair on my arms.

With the power of retrospection, I could admit it to myself. I'd never been remotely interested in Ricky. Not before our engagement, not after, and certainly not now. Oh, my pride had been wounded by his rejection. I'd pinned certain hopes and dreams on our metaphorical wedding, but the delay in planning was a true reflection of my lack of interest in what came next—the marriage. When I'd thought of my future the only thing I'd ever felt certain of was my place beside James. I'd never wanted another job. Never wanted to work with anyone but him. Even on our darkest days, when contracts fell over or suppliers tried to screw us, we'd finished the day with a laugh.

You love him. You've always loved him.

The realisation may be new, but the feelings were familiar friends. Like a prodigal son returning from lands afar, attraction began to build in my belly.

"Oh, Hazel," I whispered, wrapping arms around myself. "What have you done?"

I'd hurt him. Rejected the man who had done nothing but love me for who I was. And now, when I was finally in a place to admit that to myself and to him, he'd disappeared.

"Would I marry him if I didn't have to worry about the company?"

I closed my eyes, searching my gut for an answer.

Yes.

A weight lifted from my shoulders.

I need to let go of the past. Dad is gone. The company is better off in the hands of someone who cares for it and knows what to do with it.

I looked out at the water that lapped quietly at the shore, the moon reflecting off the inky black depths.

And I deserve happiness.

Decision made, I pulled out my phone, sending off a text.

HAZEL

Where are you? Come home, we need to talk.

I waited, hoping he might reply. After long minutes I sighed, shaking my head and tucking the phone away once more.

With a heavy heart, I looked out at the lake, shivering in the cool breeze.

"Where are you, James?"

CHAPTER 10

James

"Have you found anything?"

Around the table, my siblings and our team of forensic accountants shook their heads.

"Nothing yet."

"Nope."

I blew out a breath, threading fingers through my hair. "Keep looking."

The clock on the wall ticked over to the early hours of the morning, our work fuelled by coffee and day-old donuts.

I'd left Hazel at the lake and returned to the house only to find Ash and Millie sun baking. Sensing my mood, my brother had asked one question.

"What do you need?"

It had cut through all the bullshit, forcing me to confront the barriers in my path.

"Hazel. I need Hazel."

"So, what do you need to do to get her?"

That one question had shocked me into action.

"I need to buy Bronze Pharmaceuticals."

A slow grin had spread across Ash's face. "Buy or just put in an offer so you can get your hands on their books?"

No one had ever accused my brother of being an idiot.

"How quickly can you make it happen?"

Ash had called an emergency board meeting and set out the proposal to purchase. It had been unanimously agreed that following an appraisal of the books by our financial team, we'd make an offer.

We'd called David and given him our figure —on the condition that he grant us access to the books that afternoon. The greedy fucker had jumped at our number.

I'd called in the big guns—asking my forensic accountants to work through the night to find me answers.

My phone beeped.

DOGG PACK GROUP CHAT
MOMMADOGG

How's it all going?

JAMES

Why are you guys up?

DADDYDOGG

Your sister has a fever and woke
us all up vomiting. Sam and I
are mopping up vomit while
Karen bathes our Janie.

SAMMY

She managed to yack all over
the wall and carpet on the way
to the bathroom. A truly
impressive effort.

I shook my head, grinning at my family's interaction.

"Poor Janeane," Jay muttered from his spot at the table. "Must be that bug going around their school."

Jay and Ryan sat at the table, assisting the accountants. They weren't number wizards, but they could file and print and categorise with the best of them—something we desperately needed at stupid o'clock in the morning.

I shot off a text to my family.

JAMES

It's still going. Nothing yet.

ASH

FYI, Hazel's just gone to bed. I'll
text again in the morning when
she's up.

Ash had wanted to come and help, and
considering my brother was an actual
goddamned genius, I'd have loved his
assistance. But I needed this to happen without
tipping Hazel off. I needed to work out how to
save her company.

"Mr. Dogg?"

I turned to find my head accountant
standing behind me, his expression one of
confusion.

"Hit me, Tim."

"I'm sorry to interrupt, sir. It's just...."
He hesitated, looking down at the sheet of
paper in his hands. "I think I found
something."

I took the offered papers, settling at the
table to begin reading over the figures.

I tapped one of the highlighted figures.
"This is a shit-ton of money coming out each
month. What's the expenditure?"

He shook his head. "That's just it. We can't
find anything."

Red flags began to wave in my head.

"Say more."

He shrugged. "There are invoices, but the

company doesn't exist. We can't find a trace
of it."

"So, who owns the account?"

"We don't know."

I stared at the paper in my hands, mentally
tallying the numbers.

"Tim?"

"Yes?"

"Can you get me the number for the
financial ombudsman's office?" I looked up to
find him staring at me, his eyes wide.

"The—" He swallowed. "You think this is
fraud?"

I have my suspicions.

"Just get me the number."

He moved off, and I looked back down at
the paper in my hands.

Where there's smoke, there's fire.

Ryan and Jay took the seats on either side
of me, their bodies leaning in as they looked at
the paper in my hands.

"I'm gonna be honest," Jay said, tapping the
sheet. "I don't understand a word of this shit,
but I'm glad you do."

I chuckled, giving him a shoulder bump.
"You don't have to understand anything except
the zeros in your bank account."

"Which get bigger every day thanks to you
and Ash."

Jay had fronted our seed money for the business. When we'd finally made it big, we'd handed him back all his cash with interest and shares in the company. He was the Wood in Dogg Wood Industries, and, despite his protests, Ash and I wouldn't have it any other way.

"What are you thinking?" Ryan asked, his fingers tapping on the desk.

"That the police will investigate, and they'll work it out, one way or another."

Ryan rolled his eyes. "You're a better man than me. I'd take it to the media."

I considered my sibling, reminded of just how young he really was. The kid might be at college, but he wasn't operating in the real world just yet.

"A trial by media isn't going to win him Hazel, or win a trial." Jay stood, stretching to his full height, his back cracking loudly. "Are we done here?"

I glanced around the table, the accountants were still working on the remainder of the papers.

"You guys go, I'll finish up."

Ryan shook his head. "In for a pup, in for a pound. That's the Dogg way."

I rolled my eyes. "That is *not* a saying."

"Is too. I made it up."

My phone vibrated with an incoming text. I looked down at the screen, my heart seizing at the new text from Hazel.

HAZEL

I miss you.

My fingers hovered over my screen as I struggled to decide how to respond.

JAMES

You should be asleep.

I waited, my body tense as I watched the three little dots, waiting for her reply.

HAZEL

I can't.

JAMES

Why not?

HAZEL

The bed feels empty
without you

I froze, my cock hardening as I read and reread her message.

JAMES

I don't understand.

HAZEL

Come home and I'll explain. This
isn't a conversation for text.

I looked around the room at the tired faces.

"Let's call it a night," I said, standing up.
"Everyone get some sleep. We'll start again
tomorrow."

I grabbed my jacket as Tim came over, a
slip of paper in his hand.

"Here's the number."

"Thanks." I tucked it into my pocket. "And
thanks for your work today."

"Any time, boss. You know that."

I clapped him on the shoulder, moving to
the meeting room door.

"Yo, bro?"

I paused in the doorway, glancing back to
where Jay and Ryan stood, both of them with
their arms crossed, massive grins on their faces.

"What?"

Jay laughed, sending a thumbs up. "Tell her
welcome to the family."

CHAPTER 11

James

Hazel stood at the edge of the deck in short pajama pants and a baggy blue shirt. The light of dawn just beginning to tint the sky as she turned to me, her hair shining in the light.

I stopped at the stairs, watching her as she stared out at the lake.

She's never looked more beautiful.

It was the same thought I had every time I saw her. It was why my favourite days were any that contained Hazel.

I love this woman.

I stepped up and onto the deck, managing to hit every creaky stair and plank along the way.

"I can hear you," Hazel said, her voice containing a thread of humour. She looked back over her shoulder, offering me a small grin. "Come join me."

I walked up beside her, leaning on the rail, unable to stop my body from finding contact with hers. My arm pressed against her arm, the side of my hip against her hip, I wanted more and yet it wasn't enough.

"What did your text mean?" I asked as I took my place beside her, both of us staring out at the water.

She leaned into me, her thighs pressing again mine.

"Just what I said, the bed felt empty without you."

There was no teasing in her tone.

"Hazel...."

She turned fully towards me, lifting one hand to place it on it my chest.

"James, I have something to tell you."

My dick hardened, my control stretched to the limit as I fought every instinct that said to lean in and kiss her.

She tilted her head back, her gaze searching my face. "You're my best friend."

Fuck. Friend zoned.

"And I love you as a friend."

I fucking knew it.

"But here's the thing. I can't think of you as *just* a friend anymore."

See? You should have made a move, you douchebag. She—wait. What?

I stared down at Hazel, unable to process her words.

"You can't—I—say that again?"

She grinned, her body sinking into mine.

"You're right, James. You're my happily ever after. When you enter a room my heart skips. When you're not there I look for you. You're the tea to my toast. The peanut to my jelly. There's nothing I want more than to wake up with you every day." She laughed, reaching up to cup my cheeks. "Preferably without a pillow wall between us."

My arms automatically went around her, holding this woman close. In my shock I could only stare at her, my mouth agape.

"Say something," she whispered after a moment.

"But what about your dad's company?"

A cloud passed over her, some of the light dimming.

"Everything has to come to an end. I can't run the company. And I can't expect my chosen partner to prop up a failing business. It's not meant to come to me until my thirtieth birthday but I'm going to ask David to sell it.

It's the best option for everyone. Hopefully, someone who understands the industry will acquire it and build Bronze Pharmaceuticals up to what it was."

I stepped back, pulling the sheet from my pocket, the post-it with the ombudsman's number stuck to the front, and handed it to her.

"Hazel, Dogg Wood Industries made an offer on your business yesterday. We wanted to acquire it. We found evidence of suspected fraud." I tapped the post-it. "I think David's laundering money through an offshore account. That's where your trust went."

She sucked in a breath, her face paling.

"All you need to do is call the ombudsman and lodge a complaint."

Her hands trembled as she looked down at the papers in her hands.

"Why did you do this?"

A weird sense of bittersweet regret pooled in my belly. "Because I want you to have choices, Hazy. I want you to have everything you've ever dreamed of. I want to give you everything."

She looked up, a frown marring her brow. "But all I want is you."

I stared at her for a beat. "You're sure?"

"Yes! I'm in love with you—sexual, long-lasting, totally satisfying, and not at all platonic love!"

The dam walls broke and a tidal wave of need crashed through my body.

"Fuck!"

I swept her up in my arms, our bodies crushing together as finally, after decades of wanting our mouths met and I got my first taste of Hazel.

Per-fucking-fection.

CHAPTER 12

Hazel

Oh. My. God.

It was the best kiss I'd ever had. Any kiss that had come before felt like a pale imitation of James' kiss. The man didn't kiss so much as devour.

James pulled back, a whimper escaping me at the loss of his mouth.

"You sure?" he asked, his voice hoarse.

"Positive." I reached up, threading fingers in his hair. "Less talk, more kiss."

"No, Hazy. If we do this then we do this right. I want everything. I want you at work and in my bed. I want your snuggles and laughter. I want amazing sex and incredible memories. It's you and me, Hazel, forever."

"What are you saying?"

"I want you to marry me."

Hysterical laughter bubbled up my throat. "We haven't even had sex yet."

"Who needs sex when we have a lifetime of memories?"

"I mean, my clitoris would like a little attention," I spluttered.

A sexy as sin grin stole across his lips, robbing me of my breath. "Oh, I think I can do something about that."

One hand roamed down my body to cut my pussy through my pajama shorts, my body bowed at his possessive touch.

"Yes, you'll marry me?" he asked, his breathing harsh.

"Yes," I answered, taking a leap of faith. "Yes, I'll marry you.

He kissed me immediately, his arms wrapping around my body, his mouth hot and wet and oh so possessive.

And that hand. That naughty hand with its wicked fingers slipped inside my shorts, finding my skin and sliding down to gently play with my clit.

More.

As if he had heard my thoughts, James boosted me up, setting me on the rickety deck railing to step between my legs, his fingers continuing to stroke me.

"James, what are you—"

He silenced me with a punishing kiss, his hefty body crowding me in.

"No. More. Arguments." He told me between kisses. "You're mine."

The word mine sent my desire spiralling. Heat spread through my body like warm honey.

"You gonna come for me, pretty girl?"

I groaned against his mouth as he stroked me, his fingers exploring me with a possessive but reverent touch.

"James...."

I arched back as my climax hit, my body exploding with pent-up desire.

Oh, crabapples!

James held me as I turned into a puddle of satisfied glop, the morning sun already beginning to warm my back.

As I came back to myself, I became aware of one very big, very hard, very hot appendage pressing against me.

"Should we take this inside?" I asked my body heating once again at the thought of him inside me.

"You sure you want to—"

I silenced his protest with a kiss. With a possessive initiative I hadn't realised I owned, I wrapped my legs around his hips, grinding myself on him. James groaned, his hands skimming the side of my body to come up and cup my breasts.

"Fucking love your tits," he grunted against my lips. "That red dress you own drives me fucking crazy every time you wear it. I just want to undo the halter straps and bear you to the world, forcing them to watch while I suck on them, marking you as mine."

Oh, yes please.

My hips bucked at his filthy words, my body desperate for release.

With a curse, James lifted me, my limbs clutching at him as he stalked into the house, carrying me passed a staring Dylan and Meredith.

"About bloody time," Dylan laughed, giving me a little wave.

"Should we save some breakfast?" Meredith called as James shoved open the door to our bedroom.

"Yes. We'll have it for lunch."

I shivered at James' possessive tone.

"Are you sure? Breakfast is the most important meal of the day."

James kicked the door shut with his foot, locking out the world as he stared down at me.

"I already have a feast."

His feral expression was so unlike anything that I'd ever seen before that for a moment I forgot this was someone I'd known for years. I forgot that I'd seen him with braces, and he'd seen me in blue eyeliner. I forgot that we'd experienced acne and growth spurts and awkward phases together.

I forgot everything except how much my body, my heart, my soul wanted him.

"Make love to me."

With a feral grin, he dropped me on the bed, falling to the floor to place his mouth over the cotton of my shorts. I whimpered, the teasing heat of his mouth both too much and not enough.

"Drenched," he muttered, his hands slipping under my shirt to cup my breast. "You can't fake what's between us."

Why would I even want to try?

I'd done that. I'd done the false love story with Ricky. Oh, we'd never consummated anything. I could barely bring myself to kiss his cheek when required.

The real thing has always been here. He's always been here.

I ripped off my shirt, desperate to be skin-to-skin with this incredible man.

"Oh, fuck. Hazel."

He crawled up the bed to suck my breasts, worshipping one then the other as I tried to concentrate on getting him naked. Neither of us was winning the battle.

"Lord have mercy," I whispered, my eyelids fluttering shut as he began to press kisses along the sensitive underside of my breasts. "You're far too good at this."

"I've had years to imagine this, babe."

"And practice."

He chuckled darkly, rocking back on his knees to fist my sleep shorts. "Practice? Fuck no. You're my first and only, darlin'. I knew that from the time I was old enough to fist my own cock."

With one move he whipped off my shorts, leaving me naked and stunned under him.

"You're a—"

Anything I'd been about to say faded away as his talented mouth covered mine once more.

I could feel how wet I was as need slicked the sensitive skin of my inner thighs. James shifted, his rough fingers sliding through my wet heat to part me, his thumb finding my clit.

"Oh yeah," he whispered against my lips as he began to draw circles. "You're gonna be a good little girl for me, aren't you?"

That shouldn't be hot. Why is that hot?

I leaned forward, my teeth digging into his shoulder as his teasing fingers played my body.

"That's it, baby girl. Let me take care of you. Let me play with your sweet little clit. Let me make you feel better."

"Oh!"

My body shuddered, his fingers stroking me to a lusty, loud climax.

"James!"

"Again?" He whispered against my ear, his body still clothed and hard above mine.

I nodded, incapable of speaking.

With a hungry chuckle, he rocked back, stripping the clothes from his body.

Oh. My. God.

His cock fell free, heavy and girthy, thick and long, the length of him bouncing once before dipping.

The man is... he's...

My spirit left my body.

"I'm gonna be dicked to death."

CHAPTER 13

James

I chuckled, enjoying her shocked gaze.

I was a big guy—it only made sense that my cock matched the rest of me. Sure, I wasn't the longest guy out there, but I had thickness going for me.

Though, by the look in Hazel's eye, she was happy with what she had to work with.

I fisted my dick, using some precum to glide over my length as I began to jerk myself roughly.

"Do you like to watch, pretty girl?"

I relished the way Hazel shuddered at my words.

Fucking perfect for me.

"Can I taste?"

I blinked, my hand stilling. "Taste?"

She reached out, one finger catching a drop of precum.

Fuuuuuuuck.

I shifted up the bed, coming to settle over her, positioning my cock so it was at her mouth level.

"Taste me, Hazel."

Her eyelids fell to half-mast as her tongue flicked out gently, lapping at my cock.

"Fuck." My head fell back as my hips twitched; a near-overpowering need to fuck her mouth hitting me.

Pull it to-fucking-gether, James. You need to make this good.

Just as I was about to draw back, Hazel lifted her head from the bed, her mouth closing around the crown of my cock.

Abort! Abort!

I pulled back, her mouth releasing my cock with a pop.

"What—?"

"Fuck, I need to be in you."

I moved to the bedside table, digging in the drawer for a condom. "Fuck."

Hazel rolled her eyes, leaning over the side of the bed to find her toiletry bag. From it, she pulled a strip of condoms.

My jaw gritted, jealousy raging at the thought of her using them with anyone else.

"Don't worry," she whispered, reaching up to run fingers over my cheek. "I stole them from Millie. I figured neither of us would have anything."

"You didn't...?"

She shook her head, a slight flush heating her cheeks. "My one and only adventure with penetration was with a silicon toy a few years ago. I'm afraid I'm just as inexperienced as you."

I stared at her for a beat, possessive delight surging through me turning my need to kiss every inch of her into a desire to mark.

"You're never escaping me now." I kissed her, nipping at her lips, our tongues tangling as I stole the condoms from her grasp, ripping a packet open to roll one down my length.

"Ready, baby girl?" I asked as she wiggled under me.

"Yes!"

Chuckling, I began to rub my cock up and down her slit, teasing us both.

"James!"

I found her entrance, lining myself up. With one final kiss, I eased myself in, both of us groaning at the delicious intrusion.

Tight, hot, mine.

"Fuck, baby girl, you're the most incredible thing I've ever felt."

"You're... you're...." She moaned, her greedy little whimpers driving me wild.

I fucking love this woman.

I pulled back a fraction then began to rock against her, working my cock into her tight little channel, stretching her around me.

"Okay?" I asked desperately trying to think of anything but how incredible Hazel felt.

"Oh, yes." Her breathy little sigh of delight hit me in the gut.

"Ready?"

"Yes."

I began to thrust,

I settled into a slow glide, gritting my teeth as she gasped, clenching around me.

"Fuck you feel incredible, baby girl," I grunted, drawing this out, never wanting this to end.

She's mine. All mine.

"James, I need... I need..."

Oh, I know exactly what you need.

I picked up my pace, beginning to feed her my dick in one hard, fast thrust that sent the bed clattering against the wall.

Over and over, thrust after thrust, I built Hazel up, until finally, with a shift of my hips to change the angle, she exploded, screaming and clawing at me, her little teeth nipping at the skin at my neck while her sweet pussy squeezed my dick like a fucking vice.

I lost all sense of fucking control. I came, my head thrown back, a roar echoing through the house as I emptied myself into the woman who owned me—mind, body, and soul.

We collapsed on the bed, and I rolled us, snuggling her close, determined not to crush the love of my life.

I'm gonna need to wrap her in cotton wool and keep her locked up, barefoot, and pregnant for all eternity. I can't live life without you, baby girl.

For a long moment, we lay panting together, our skin cooling, reveling in the aftermath.

"James?"

"Mm?" I turned slightly, pressing a kiss to her forehead.

"Can I ask a favor?"

"Anything," I promised. "You want it, I'll make sure it happens."

"Next time, can we please have sex in a room without creepy doll wallpaper?"

A startled laugh burst from my chest, my laughter shaking the bed as I rolled over to hover above her.

"Absolutely not," I said, nuzzling her neck. "I can't wait that long."

She blew out a sigh, tipping her head to one side to grant me better access. "Guess I'll just have to get used to it then."

"Unless you're up for shower sex?"

She opened one eye, giving me a sassy grin. "I could do shower sex. I've always wanted to try the doggy position."

"Babe," I hauled her up and into my arms, carrying her towards the ensuite. "You're marrying a Dogg—every position is the doggy position."

CHAPTER 14

Hazel

We emerged from our love cocoon some time in the early afternoon. Exhausted, body still buzzing with aftershocks and the remaining tingles of desire, my only thought was to fill my belly.

And not die of embarrassment.

Out on the deck sat the whole Dogg Pack minus James' eldest brother, Hayden, who was on vacation with his wife.

I stumbled to a halt, blinking at the crowd outside.

"Did you invite your family?"

"Fuck no." James scrubbed a hand across his face. "Shit. I should have known."

"Known what?"

He wrapped an arm around my neck, pulling me into him gently. "That they'd want to come and welcome you to the family. And check that you're okay after the whole David might be a criminal thing."

I shrugged off that issue, knowing it would need to be dealt with but it could wait for at least another day.

"Do you think they heard us?"

"Oh, they did."

James and I jumped, both of us startled as Meredith sat up from where she'd been lying on the couch.

"Meredith! What the fuck?"

She placed a hand on the velour. "I like the feel of this material."

"Don't let Dylan hear you saying that."

She nodded at the crowd on the deck. "They arrived just as you began coitus in the shower. I encouraged them to move outside. They agreed."

A blush began to burn my cheeks. "Um, thank you."

"No problem." She lay back down, disappearing from view. "There's food on the table outside."

James led me through the house, sending me a *she's weird* look.

I nodded, answering with a *but I like her* grin.

"Here they are!" Jay spread his arms wide, his grin massive. "The happy couple!"

Kill me now.

After a round of hugs and kisses, we settled at the table, beginning to work our way through heaped plates of ribs, rolls, salads, and delicious cheeses.

"Not to bring the tone down," Ash said, absently playing with Millie's hair. "But what *are* you gonna do about that discrepancy, Hazel?"

I swallowed a mouthful of meat and then gently dabbed at my lips. "Report him. I don't have any other choice."

James reached out, threading our fingers together and squeezing mine.

"Ouch," Keiko, Millie's best friend, said with a wince. "That has to be a hard decision, reporting your own stepdad."

"Surprisingly, no. He's not only stealing from me; he's stealing from our employees." I glanced over at James. "Good bosses take care of their people. They respect them and kill themselves to ensure the company is financially viable, sustainable, and working to better their lives."

He sent me a look that said he was ready for dessert.

I sent him a look that said I was more than prepared to *be* dessert.

"Good points."

Ryan raised his glass. "A toast to good bosses, great friends, and our newly engaged couple."

"And to finally popping that cherry," Jay said with a laugh, tipping his cup at James.

"Fuck you, man."

"Language boys!" Will bellowed, cupping Janie's ears. "Your sister is present."

"Oh, please." Karen rolled her eyes. "As if you don't say worse at home."

"I would never!"

As I sipped my drink, I looked around the table, my heart overflowing with love for this wonderful family.

"You sure you're ready for this?" James asked, tilting his head towards the boisterous crew.

"Wild dogs couldn't drag me away."

He leaned in to kiss me just as Sam rebutted my answer.

"Drag you away? Us wild Dogg's want to make you part of the pack."

I laughed, pulling back from James with a grin. "And I wouldn't have it any other way."

EPILOGUE ONE

Hazel

Five months later

In a weird sense of déjà vu, I stared at the article on my screen. Stunned shock rendering me speechless.

I didn't think this would ever happen.

My phone rang, and without thinking I slid my thumb across the screen to answer the call.

"Hello?"

"Hazel, did you see the news?" James' voice was strong and reassuring.

"I'm looking at it right now."

"He did it, Hazel. David's going to jail."

I knew it wasn't quite that clean-cut. There would be a trial and no doubt appeals, but with all the evidence the investigators had uncovered, one thing was for sure—David wasn't likely to be sleeping in his own bed any time soon.

I cleared my throat. "It doesn't say what's going to happen to the company."

"I've heard that the board is already convening an emergency meeting. I suspect they'll try and offload it." My fiancé cleared his throat. "Do you want me to buy it for you?"

A small part of me wanted it. I wanted the memory of my dad to be kept alive. I wanted his legacy to flourish.

But then, a company wasn't his legacy, I was.

"No. Thank you, though." I grinned, leaning back in my chair. "You know, it still freaks me out that you can buy and sell small countries with one click."

"Speaking of, how do you feel about an island? I was thinking we should buy an island for our honeymoon. Private, completely secluded, no family or press intruding uninvited."

I laughed. "Absolutely not. We don't need an island."

"Does anyone? What's the point of being rich if not to indulge sometimes?"

"Hmm, maybe to help others?"

"Psh," his voice came from behind me. I turned in my seat, my heart skipping as I saw him exit the executive elevator. "Why help others when I can spoil you?"

I hung up, smoothing my skirt down as I stood. "I don't know, karma? Being a good human being? Trying to beat Bill Gates?"

He wrapped one arm around my waist, pulling me into him. "Bill Gates? Please. If I was going into philanthropy, I'd aspire to be Mackenzie Scott. That woman is an icon."

I giggled, raising up on tiptoe to kiss him. "Missed you."

"Missed you more." He sighed. "When is our wedding, again?"

"Two hundred and forty-three days away."

"Too long."

"Tell that to the wedding planner."

We both glanced over at Dylan's desk, finding them glaring at the two of us.

"Abso-fucking-lutely not." They crossed their arms over their chest. "I'm already stretched to get everything planned in time; I'm not going to jeopardize the vision we've created because you two want to share a surname."

I swallowed a laugh. "We love you, Dylan."

"You bloody better with the work I'm putting into this wedding."

James caught my chin, lifting my head. "Love you, pretty girl."

I melted into him. "Love you more."

"You sure? I remember when I was pining for you for a few years while you—"

I cut him off with a kiss, relishing the taste of his laughter.

EPILOGUE TWO

James

Two hundred and forty-three days later

"You may kiss the bride!"

Fucking finally.

I yanked Hazel into me, ignoring the laughter of our guests, desperate to taste her joy.

Our lips crashed together, the kiss deep and delicious—exactly how the first kiss as a married couple should be.

We pulled back; our foreheads pressed together as we grinned at each other.

"You can't escape now."

She laughed, squeezing me tight. "Neither can you."

Why would I ever want to?

The rest of the day passed in a blurb of photos, handshakes, hugs, and toasts—including some that were best forgotten.

"And so," Jay said, wrapping up what had to be both the best and worst groomsman speech in the history of the world. "Let's all raise our glasses to the happy couple. May Hazel love you forever—" The bastard paused for dramatic effect. "—because none of us want to do this again."

The crowd laughed, raising their glasses in a toast.

"To Hazel and James!"

"And now," Dylan, who also happened to be our MC for the evening, said into the microphone. "The couple will have their first dance."

I led Hazel onto the dancefloor as the band began to play *A Thousand Years.*

As I swayed with my wife in my arms, all I could think about was how much I deeply loved my Hazel.

"Thank you," she whispered as we circled the dance floor.

"For?"

"Waiting for me. For loving me. For creating this beautiful life with me."

In one smooth move, I spun her out and

then pulled her back in, grinning at her laughter.

"I'd always wait for you, Hazy. You're my other half."

"I love you."

Under the glittering lights, we kissed, sealing our promises to each other.

"James?"

"Yes, wife?"

"By the way, I'm pregnant."

The image of me lifting Hazel into the air, of the joy on both our faces would be the one that would grace Hazel's bedside table for years to come.

EPILOGUE THREE

Ryan

Five years later

"Shit! Shit, shit, shit!" My sister-in-law's scream echoed through the parking lot. "Just breathe, Hazel. In and out, in and out."

"Where's the ambulance?" She panted, her face red and blotchy.

That is a damned good question.

"On its way."

"And James?"

"Also, on his way."

I fucking hope.

Hazel turned her tear-glistening gaze on me. "What am I going to do, Ryan? I can't have this baby here. James hasn't missed one birth. He can't miss this one."

After three kids, you'd think he'd know better.

I looked around the parking lot of Pier Pressure, silently cursing her craving for burgers.

"Look, babies take forever, right? Don't worry too much. The ambulance will be here any—" I broke off as Hazel crushed the bones in my hand, her body bowing as she groaned through another contraction.

Fuck. That's two minutes. Fuck!

I glanced out the car window, desperately searching for someone—anyone—to help me.

"Hey! You! Help!"

The guy turned, the sun at his back blocking me from seeing him clearly.

"Me?"

"Yeah, I need towels and hot water and—" I trailed off, at a loss at what else I might require. "Can you just get them? My sister's having a baby!"

"Shit! I'm on it."

The guy sprinted off as I turned back to Hazel, finding her gripping her knees, her body curved up.

"Ryan—I think she's—"

"Fuck!" I bent, flicking up her skirts, nearly

passing out at the sight of a head coming out of her vagina.

Dear gods above. Women choose to do this? Fuck, I'm gonna be sick. No, you got this, Ryan. You have to have this. Hold it together, dude! HOLD IT TOGETHER!

Hazel let out a long, low groan, straining as I got into position, ready to catch the baby.

Distantly I heard a car skidding to a halt behind me as Hazel panted through another long contraction.

This will be fine. All will be fine. Everything is fine. Everything is—

"Hazel!" My brother's bellow had me sagging in relief.

"Oh, thank fucking Christ." I shifted from my kneeling position. "Hurry, James!"

My brother elbowed me out of the way, arriving in time to catch his daughter as she slid silently into the world.

For a second, my heart caught, fear striking deep when she didn't stir.

"Shit! Is she—"

Just as I was about to ask if she was okay, the baby began to squirm, her little limbs moving as she sucked in her first, deep breath. Her red face screwed up, her tiny rose bud mouth opening to let out an angry scream.

"Oh! Wow!" A hand pressed to my back as I stared at my niece. "Here are your towels."

Linen was pressed into my arms, which I took automatically and used to wrap my niece while James cared for Hazel.

"Hey there, little bubba," I cooed, the sounds of emergency sirens beginning to wail in the background. "You're gonna be an absolute firecracker, aren't you? Arriving so quickly and with such anger! Don't worry, babe. I'll help you slay all those dragons."

I looked up, finding Hazel watching me, tears in her eyes.

"You ready to hold her, Momma?"

She nodded, reaching out for her newest addition. I placed my niece in her arms and stepped back, watching as the family began to bond even as the paramedics swarmed the scene.

"Excuse me, can you move, please? We need to create a bit of space here." One of the paramedics waved me back.

Where were you five minutes ago, dude?

"Great catch, Ryan. Holding a baby suits you."

I froze, my entire body turning to ice. Slowly, I turned, coming face-to-face with the man who'd broken my heart five years ago.

"Trent?"

He held out one of the towels. "You have some blood on your arms."

I looked down, noting the red lines. "Oh, right. Thanks."

I considered him as I scrubbed my skin. He had the same good looks, athletic build and wild hair he'd left the Cove with all those years ago.

Why does he look so good?

He doesn't. He's the embodiment of the devil, remember?

He tilted his head to one side. "You look good, Ryan."

And you look like an Ex I never want to see again.

"Thanks," I muttered, aware that he'd caught me in what had to possibly the third worst way to reconnect with an ex. "What are you doing in town?"

"I've moved back."

My gaze whipped up to meet his. "Excuse me?"

"Yeah."

"I... well, welcome back, I guess."

Fuck. I guess I better start shopping for one-way tickets to Australia. Are they sending people to the moon yet? What about Mars?

Trent tilted his head to one side, a small

grin playing on his lips. "Guess we'll be seeing a lot of each other from now on."

"I don't know about that; Capricorn Cove has really grown since you last lived here."

"Ryan! We need you."

I turned to walk away, calling over my shoulder. "Bye Trent."

"See you soon, Ryan."

Over my dead body.

———

Thank you so much for reading Pier Pressure!

You can continue the entire series by checking them out on my website at
www.EvieMitchell.com

*If you enter the code **EBOOK10** you can get 10% off your purchase from my website.*

ABOUT THE AUTHOR

Hey, I'm Evie Mitchell.
I'm a thirty-something romance author (she/her/hers) living with disability. I believe in inclusion, accessibility, and fierce romance. My loves include steamy romance novels, my sexy husband, our THREE sausage dogs (THE FUR!!!), and my ever-growing collection of book-related mugs.

As a woman with a diverse work history, including in areas such as hospitality, retail, emergency response, event management, human rights, disability access, and security— my books are filled with true stories (bridezillas), worst-case scenarios (malfunctioning zippers), and my favorite tropes (one-bed).

I'm a strong proponent of #OwnVoices, and specialize in fiercely inclusive happily ever afters.

EvieMitchell.com
Socials: @EvieMitchellAuthor

As You Wish
You Sleigh Me
Meat Load
Resolution Revolution

Dogg Pack
Puppy Love
Bad English
The Frock Up
Trick or Trent
New Year's Faye

Reigning Hearts
The Marriage Claim
Silent Knight

Men of Trinity Bay
Kink in the Road

Nameless Souls MC
Runner
Wrath
Ghost
Shield

Elliot Security

Rough Edge
Bleeding Edge